Dedicated to Louis Archuleta. A man who taught me to celebrate and respect all things different, especially ourselves.

**Louie was a burn victim and almost died at the age of 10. He never let the scars make him self conscious and instead used them to be an example to help other people transcend their insecurities.*

Let happiness bloom in the freshness of your mind.
In the gentle wind of your thoughts.
On the ground of kindness and compassion.
-Debasish Mridha

MATH!

TODAY IS SWEET PEA'S FIRST DAY OF SCHOOL. SHE IS A LITTLE NERVOUS ABOUT MEETING THE OTHER CHILDREN.

CORN WAS THE FIRST CLASSMATE SHE MET.
HE SAID, "YOU'RE NOT VERY STRONG ARE YOU?"

SWEET PEA SAID, "YES I AM!"
AND TRIED TO SHOW CORN HER STRENGTH.

THEN PEAR CAME UP AND SAID,
"NOT MUCH ON YOUR BOTTOM HALF IS THERE?"

2+2=4
4+4=8

AND AGAIN, SWEET PEA TRIED TO CHANGE HERSELF TO PLEASE PEAR.

NEXT, BEANSTALK SAID,
"MY, YOU'RE QUITE SHORT."

SHHH
PLEASE

"NO, I'M NOT!" SAID SWEET PEA.
AND TRIED TO STRETCH AS HIGH AS SHE COULD.

WHEN SWEET PEA WAS ALONE IN THE HALL,
SHE STARTED TO CRY.
SHE THOUGHT OF ALL THE THINGS SHE
WASN'T
AND ALL THE THINGS SHE
COULDN'T DO.
SHE WAS AFRAID SHE WOULD NEVER
FIT IN WITH THE OTHER VEGETABLES.

JUST THEN,
THE OTHER VEGGIE KIDS WALKED UP.
"WHY ARE YOU CRYING?" THEY ASKED.
"WELL," SAID SWEET PEA, "I'M DIFFERENT
AND I THOUGHT YOU WOULDN'T LIKE ME."
"SWEET PEA, WE LIKE YOU
BECAUSE
YOU'RE DIFFERENT!"

THIS MADE SWEET PEA BEAM WITH PRIDE.
SHE KNEW THERE WASN'T ANOTHER
SWEET PEA JUST LIKE HER ANYWHERE. AND
THAT WAS SOMETHING SHE COULD DO
THAT NOBODY ELSE COULD.

THE END

Made in the USA
Lexington, KY
03 April 2016